THE TASTE *OF* HER

AIKEN PONDER

WORDS TO PONDER PUBLISHING COMPANY, LLC

First printing, 2026

Address inquiries to Aiken Ponder

Printed in the United States of America

For more information, email Aiken.Ponder@gmail.com

Book Designer: Rasel Khondokar

Cover Designer: Victoria Davies

ISBN (eBook): 979-8-89664-017-2

ISBN (paperback): 979-8-89664-018-9

ISBN (hardcover): 979-8-89664-019-6

Words to Ponder Publishing Company, LLC

Chagrin Falls, Ohio

www.wordstoponderpublishing.com

For the women who were taught to fold their wings —

and unfolded them anyway.

And to the ones who steady me when I fly.

Some hungers are not about wanting more.

They're about wanting yourself.

Contents

Prologue

Twenty Years Prior

Music drifted through the room, low and unhurried, settling into the air like something that did not need permission to stay. Reighn felt it first in her shoulders, then lower, beneath her ribs, where warmth spread with a patience that made her shift her weight without realizing she had.

The light was amber and forgiving, softening edges until even stillness looked intentional. She stood near the bar with an untouched drink sweating against her palm, watching people move as if they had already decided no one in the room required impressing. Laughter rose and thinned. A woman leaned back into her partner's chest, eyes closed, her mouth parting slightly as hands slid along her waist.

That was what caught Reighn.

Not the touch.

The ease.

Journey nudged her shoulder. "Girl, you okay?"

Reighn nodded, but her breath had deepened and stayed that way. She wasn't overwhelmed. She wasn't startled. Something in her had simply woken and refused to lie back down.

Someone brushed past her, soft fabric grazing bare skin at her arm, the contact lingering a fraction longer than accident required. An apology followed, low and warm, edged with a salt-sweet scent that did not smell like perfume so much as skin. It stayed with her. It moved lower.

Her body responded before she could discipline it, heat tightening at her center with the familiarity of something long practiced and carefully contained. The recognition of it startled her more than the sensation itself. Wanting did not feel foreign. It felt remembered.

Across the room, a man met her gaze and did not look away immediately. His eyes traveled, unhurried, down the line of Reighn's collarbone before returning to her mouth. No smile. No invitation. Just awareness.

Reighn held the look for a breath longer than she normally would.

The warmth in her stomach sharpened.

She set the glass down.

"I think I need air," she said, though she was already moving.

Outside, the night pressed cool against skin that still held the room's heat. She bent forward, palms braced against her thighs, breath spilling out in a quiet laugh that felt less like embarrassment and more like release. The sensation did not fade with the distance from the music. It remained, steady and insistent, as if it had been waiting for her to stop pretending it was not there.

It wasn't what she had seen that unsettled her.

It was the way her body had answered.

And she had not expected the answer to feel so certain.

Chapter One

From the floor-to-ceiling windows of her living room, the sun rises over the Brooklyn Bridge as cargo boats move through the water below.

Reighn watches the light shift across the glass.

Olympia never disappoints.

Nestled in historic DUMBO—Down Under the Manhattan Bridge Overpass—steps from her studio and favorite cafés, it isn't just her home. It's where she lives the life she built.

When she and Sloan first toured the condo, he was captivated by the nineteen-foot ceilings. At seven foot two, ceilings mattered to him. For Reighn, it was the view.

Sloan stepped behind her that afternoon, long arms circling her as she stood at the windows. She leaned back into him, the crown of her head resting against his chest.

"If you love it," he'd said quietly, his voice rumbling above her, "we'll make it ours."

From the moment they met, something about him held her attention—not just the striking blend of Lenny Kravitz and Idris Elba, but his stillness. In rooms full of people vying for him, his attention didn't wander.

Sloan didn't do half-presence. He chose you—and acted like it.

She exhales and turns back to the laptop resting on a koa-wood tray across her bare legs. The morning light stretches along her thighs before sliding higher, warm and unhurried, and she shifts the tray as the heat settles deeper.

In a few weeks, she will open *Black Salt*. The city is already buzzing.

WABC-TV.

WNET.

1010 WINS.

"Are you on the guest list for New York's hottest art show?" the announcer says. "Baby, everyone who's anyone will be there."

She smiles.

A tomboy from East Point, Georgia—escorted home more times than she could count for tagging abandoned warehouse walls—now owns Palimpsest, one of DUMBO's most respected galleries. Mimi's rascal of a daughter. The girl who once told a police officer, Right now, I'm giving East Point my art for free. One day they'll pay for it.

Her phone vibrates. Before the second ring, she taps speaker.

"This is Reighn," she says, flipping her planner open and jotting a note beside a new artist's name.

At the other end: water against stone. Birds. The silence stretches.

"Hello?" she says, pen hovering over the page.

A voice finally comes through—warm, melodic, edged with confidence.

The number is blocked.

"I didn't expect you to answer," the woman says.

"How may I help you?" Reighn replies, closing her planner with a soft, deliberate click. She crosses one leg over the other, settling deeper into the sofa, composed.

Even as she speaks, she maps the sound.

Not Cuba. Not coastal. Mountain-city Spanish. Medellín energy.

El Poblado at dusk. The infinity pool. Sloan spinning her through the water. A helicopter ride south. Guatapé. Morning light on the lake.

He had laughed when she accused him of showing off that weekend. "You work too hard," he'd told her, pressing a kiss into her damp curls. "Let me spoil you once in a while."

She scribbles Llanogrande in the margin before realizing she's drifted.

"Hello?" she says again.

"Lo amo. Y él me ama."

I love him. And he loves me too.

The certainty in the woman's voice doesn't waver.

Calls like this happen.

Sloan had mentioned it once, almost casually. "Visibility invites commentary," he'd said softly, his lips close to hers. "We don't have to answer it."

"No lo conoces como yo. Él me dice cosas. Cosas que a ti no."

You don't know him the way I do. He tells me things. Things he doesn't tell you.

Reighn smiles faintly and taps the pen once against the tray.

"Él no sabe elegir. Así que le estoy ahorrando la incomodidad."

He doesn't know how to choose. So I'm saving him the discomfort.

Reighn waits.

"Estoy aquí. Permanentemente. Lo que decidas hacer con eso es asunto tuyo."

I'm here. Permanently. What you decide to do with that is yours.

Reighn inhales once, the smile never quite leaving.

"¿De verdad crees que el silencio te hace digna?"

Do you really think silence makes you dignified?

"I'm sure you love him," Reighn says. "And that you believe he loves you too."

The woman's breath catches.

Reighn does not shift her tone.

"Thank you for calling."

Reighn lets the quiet stretch until the line disconnects.

She writes one more note in the margin:

ceviche de camarón — shrimp in lime and heat.

She closes the planner.

Chapter Two

The chime sings. A second later, the robotic voice follows.

Front door. Opened.

Reighn checks her watch. Midmorning. The hours have slipped past. She stands and rolls the stiffness from her shoulders, arms lifting overhead before settling back into place.

Sloan steps into the kitchen, loosening his collar as he crosses the room. He slips out of his espresso Savile Row jacket and drapes it over the island stool, the slacks holding their sharp line even as he moves. His cuff links are already gone.

He kisses her right temple, then the curve just below it.

Warm. Familiar.

Then the smell reaches her.

Fried chicken. Candied yams. Mac and cheese. Cornbread wrapped in plastic stamped in black and yellow.

The Busy Bee Café.

Her mouth waters before she turns.

Smiling, he lifts the bag just beyond her grasp, the corner of his mouth tilting as she stretches for it. She presses into him without thinking, rising on her toes, her palm sliding briefly along the plane of his stomach beneath the loosened shirt.

"You didn't have to," she says, still reaching.

"I know."

She leaps. This time he lets her have it, his hands catching her at the waist as she lands, holding her there an extra beat before releasing her.

Every bite tastes like childhood kitchens and hot summers, grease on brown paper and someone calling her name from the porch. She closes her eyes once, slow, savoring.

His attention drifts to the loose pages on the counter—the ones she leaves out when she wants to think alone.

He flips one. Scans it.

"Remember the last time?" he says, folding up his sleeves. "You said the wait made it taste better."

She remembers. Tracy Gates. The second location. Sloan loving the anticipation almost as much as the meal.

His gaze shifts past her shoulder.

"What's this?"

She follows it.

The weathered portfolio. Charcoal pencils tied in chestnut leather.

Her mother had given it to her when she left for Howard. Art history first. Pratt later. Applause after that.

Sloan doesn't touch it.

"I haven't seen this since your Studio Museum days."

That internship birthed Palimpsest.

"It's time," Reighn says, sliding the portfolio closer. She sets her planner on top of it. "Before I forget why I started."

"With everything you're juggling… you're really picking this back up now?"

He unbuttons his shirt as he walks toward the stairs, fabric opening slowly over muscle she knows by heart. His body has always been easy to look at. She lets herself look.

Before Palimpsest, he called her work a hobby. Her mama's voice rises in memory, sharp and uninvited: Why you let that man name you?

Georgia Tech. Stanford. Strata Labs.

She applauds him in rooms where men are congratulated for breathing and women are asked to justify their oxygen.

He pauses at the bottom step.

"I'm meeting Ernst at The Club. Drinks and a swim."

"Have fun."

"Always."

He crosses back to her, unhurried, gathering her into him and lifting her until her feet leave the floor. Her breath catches as his mouth finds hers, deeper than a passing kiss, his hand firm at her lower back. She grips his shoulders, the press of him solid and familiar, and when he lowers her slowly, his thumb traces the inside of her waist before sliding away.

Then he takes the stairs.

A moment later, the shower starts. Sloan sings off-key, the sound echoing faintly through tile and water.

Reighn gathers her things. Planner. Pen. Folder.

Then she reaches for the scratch sheet.

Nothing.

She checks again, sliding papers aside, lifting the planner.

The page is gone.

Not misplaced.

Lifted.

Maribel Santos

Llanogrande

Ceviche de camarón

Thursday

Upstairs, the water runs.

Sloan keeps singing.

Chapter Three

Reighn steps onto Front Street and lets the cobblestones set her pace, slow at first and deliberate, her hips adjusting to the uneven rhythm as river damp curls around her ankles and the warm scent of bread drifts from Bread & Spread. Coffee grinders whine as she passes Red Coffee Stand, conversation spilling onto the sidewalk while tourists cluster near Washington Street, laughing too loudly, angling their cameras for the bridge framed just right against the sky.

She doesn't pause.

She reads a city the way others read menus, scanning for texture, for movement, for what hides between what is advertised.

Behind her, a delivery truck idles. Ahead, footsteps thin. When she turns onto Jay Street, the noise loosens its grip and the echo sharpens. Sugar and espresso give way to concrete and sun-warmed brick. By the time Burrow's pastry note ghosts the air and fades, the studio comes into view.

20 Jay Street stands solid and unshowy, warehouse bones and tall windows catching light without begging for it. It doesn't advertise art. It houses it.

Her phone vibrates just as her fingers close around her key.

She considers letting it ring.

One interruption was enough.

Then she sees the name.

"Where the hell are you?" Journey's voice carries loud enough that Reighn doesn't bother lifting the phone fully to her ear.

Journey O'Bryant. Nearest. Dearest. Mimi would have called them the Pic girls. Partners in crime.

If Reighn has a counterweight, it's Journey—sass at the surface, something steadier underneath.

"I've been sitting here half an hour."

Reighn hears the clatter of Fontainhas behind her voice, Goa's Latin Quarter transplanted into Brooklyn, loud and unapologetic.

She pivots toward the café without breaking stride.

Concrete floors worn smooth by traffic. A single slab of wood stretching the length of the bar. Floor-to-ceiling glass letting the city look in as easily as patrons look out.

Journey waves from the goldenrod sectional, already settled in like she owns the place. The server approaches before Reighn reaches the table.

"I see you started without me," Reighn says, sliding into the seat opposite her.

"Another bottle of Tinto Amorio," Journey says without looking at the server. "And another glass."

Reighn opens the menu, scans it briefly, then closes it.

"You're not getting food?" Journey asks, frowning. "I was hoping you'd get the uttapam."

Sharing is caring. Journey's favorite lie.

"Judging by the crumbs," Journey says, pointing, "Lover Boy brought you something."

Reighn glances down. Cornbread clings stubbornly to the edge of her collarbone, a faint smudge of gold against brown skin.

"He did, Nosy."

"Mr. Classy brought you food?"

"It was Busy Bee's."

Journey's delight flickers, then sharpens. "Damn."

Cheers erupt nearby as a man drops to one knee beside the window. A woman shrieks, hands flying to her mouth. Applause spreads across the café, glasses lifting in salute.

"Isn't love grand?" someone calls out.

"Another one bites the dust," Journey mutters, raising her glass.

Reighn reaches into her tote and slides a small white bag across the table.

Journey brightens instantly. "Sweet potato pie."

"When I grow up," Journey says around a bite, "I want to be just like you."

"You are grown."

"Not that grown." She peers at Reighn over the rim of her glass. "Who says, 'I want fries,' and ends up in Paris?"

Journey taps the portfolio resting against Reighn's leg. "For the record? They don't even call them fries over there."

Reighn doesn't answer.

"Oh my God." Journey wipes her fingertips on a napkin before flipping the pages. "You're painting again?"

Her voice softens as she turns the page. "These are really good."

Reighn reaches into her bag for the scratch sheet she knows should be there.

Nothing.

She checks again, fingers moving more carefully this time.

Still nothing.

For a moment she sees Sloan's hand turning pages that weren't his, lingering a second longer than necessary.

"Excuse me."

The voice is deep and low, close enough that it brushes the back of her neck before she turns.

Journey inhales through her nose, slow and dramatic, her mouth parting slightly as her eyes travel up.

"You dropped this."

A cream envelope appears beside Reighn's shoulder, sealed in dark wax that catches the light.

Cardamom rises first, then leathered iris, then sandalwood, the scent settling into the space between them and refusing to dissipate.

"Freak recognizes freak," he says, his tongue touching briefly to his lower lip before retreating.

Journey exhales sharply and snags the envelope from his hand. "Mary, Martha, Paul, and Tyrone have mercy."

The man tilts his head, his gaze never leaving Reighn. "And your name?"

"Reighn," Journey says quickly, volunteering her friend before she can answer.

"As in rain?" he asks, amusement threading through the question.

"When necessary," Reighn replies, meeting his eyes without blinking. "Otherwise, dominance."

A slow smile pulls at his mouth. "Ah hell."

Journey hands the envelope back, her fingers lingering a second longer than required.

Reighn slips it into her pocket.

"Even power needs to eat," he says. "If you decide you're ready, you'll know where to look."

He steps away without rushing.

The scent remains.

Journey fans herself with the menu. "Santal 33."

Reighn keeps her hand in her pocket, her thumb tracing the raised edge of the wax seal, pressing just hard enough to feel it hold.

Chapter Four

"Don't give me that look," Journey says, typing the last four digits into her phone and hitting save. "While you were busy buying spices, I was securing digits."

She slips the phone into her bag, posture easy, voice smooth as silk sliding over skin.

"Just because he isn't your taste doesn't mean he can't be mine," she adds. "I need a few more entries into my flavor-of-the-month club."

When they were younger, people assumed Reighn was the feisty one. Journey let them believe it. Church mouse by day. Wide eyes. Soft voice. Harmless smile. But once the streetlights flickered on, something in her sharpened and refused to dull. More than once she had called from a payphone asking Reighn to come rescue her, laughing even as sirens wailed somewhere too close.

"I keep warning you about running toward trouble," Reighn says. "Besides, what is it BigMa always said? You're too old of a cat to—"

"Oh no, you don't," Journey cuts in. "You cannot weaponize my grandmother."

"If the panties fit—"

"This doesn't apply." Journey tucks her phone deeper into her bag. "BigMa also said a woman should know the difference between chasing trouble and choosing delight." She glances back once, slow and certain. "And that is pure delight."

She loops her arm through Reighn's and sighs theatrically.

"How's the event planning?"

"Everything's coming together," Reighn says as they sidestep an older man cleaning up after his Shih Tzu. Journey crouches without hesitation, dissolving into baby talk while the dog wriggles under her touch.

"We've had several new artists submit work," Reighn continues once Journey stands again. "One in particular is stunning. Glass, brass, mixed media. It's unlike anything I've seen. I requested additional pieces. I expect everything they send to sell."

"Which," Journey says, brushing her palms along her thighs, "is exactly why I need a sneak peek."

Reighn unlocks the studio.

The room receives them quietly.

Late-afternoon light moves through tall north-facing windows, softened by sheer linen, spilling across concrete floors burnished smooth by years of work. It catches flecks of pigment and faint scars where easels once stood, resting along the edges of stacked canvases like memory returning to its place.

Oil paint lingers in the air, layered over turpentine softened by beeswax and old wood. Beneath it, a trace of incense — warm, faintly sweet.

Canvases lean against exposed brick in deliberate clusters, edges aligned but not rigid. Nothing clamors. Everything waits.

A long worktable anchors the space, scarred and honest. Brushes stand upright, clean but well-used. Sketchbooks rest spine-in. One chair remains pulled back, as though someone has just stepped away.

Even Journey lowers her voice.

"I'm so proud of you," she says. "Can you believe this? The girls who tagged anything that wouldn't run away... and now look."

Reighn moves deeper into the room.

Art has never been an accessory to her life. It steadies her pulse.

"Whoa," Journey breathes, drifting toward one of the new pieces. "It's sensual. Erotic. Sanctified and sinful at the same time."

Glass fused into brass. Fractured lines held in quiet tension. Light caught and released with intention. The work does not reach outward to be understood; it stands assured in its own knowing.

"No name?" Journey asks.

"None listed."

There is no signature in the corner. No initials carved into varnish. No mark claiming space. Only the work itself — confident enough not to narrate its presence.

Journey nods. "That's bold."

Genesis steps inside, greeting them before gesturing toward a wooden crate resting near the back wall.

"This arrived while you were out."

Journey moves toward it immediately, curiosity bright.

Reighn takes the crowbar from her gently. "Let me."

They pry the crate open together, wood giving way with a muted crack.

The piece inside shifts the air the moment the lid lifts.

Built, not painted.

Torn silk fused with resin. Charcoal pressed deep into the surface. Gold leaf catching along carved edges where material has been stripped back and returned to.

A curve suggests a hip without outlining it. A shadow deepens where a torso might turn.

"Is that a hip?" Journey asks softly.

"Implied," Reighn says. "Contained."

Genesis steps closer. "The longer you stay with it, the more intimate it becomes."

Reighn's hand lowers toward the bottom corner, and there it is — a thin, imperfect circle, deliberately broken.

Beside it, a single almond-shaped eye.

Her thumb hovers near the mark without touching it.

"The circle suggests continuity."

"The break?" Journey asks.

"Interruption," Genesis offers.

"Or choice," Reighn says.

Journey pauses, then reaches into Reighn's pocket and pulls out the cream envelope from earlier. She turns it toward the light.

The same broken circle.

The same eye.

Silence gathers, not loud, not theatrical.

"That," Journey says slowly, "feels intentional."

Reighn keeps her thumb near the break in the circle.

It does not read as damage.

It reads as decision — choice.

Chapter Five

The envelope rests on the teak table, its seal broken, slightly torn where Journey's assistance was neither requested nor required.

Reighn expected the stationery to be extraordinary. The envelope had hinted at it. What she hadn't anticipated was the scent released when the wax gave way.

Dry cedar first, clean and steady. Then something brighter — citrus without sweetness. When she lifts the flap, a third note rises. Resinous. Aged.

Not perfume.

It settles low in her throat before moving deeper.

"Mr. Smells-Delicious sends fragrant invitations too?" Journey lifts the envelope, closes her eyes, inhales.

"Isn't his name Thiago?" Reighn asks, watching as Journey folds it and slips it into her pocket like a complimentary sample.

Journey drops onto the olive-green Italian leather sofa beside her.

The Camaleonda. B&B Italia. Opening-day gift. Milan. Salone del Mobile. Reighn had protested the price. Journey dismissed her.

"For everything you've done for me? This is nothing. Besides, my butt print is going to fill more space than yours."

It does.

Inanna.

"The penmanship alone is art."

Reighn reads:

You are receiving this because you already understand restraint.

The symbol is not decoration.

It is memory.

What you do with recognition determines what happens next.

If you wish to continue the conversation, you know where to be.

Her pulse deepens instead of quickening.

Memory arrives not as images but as sensation.

A room where bodies moved without apology.

Sound carrying weight.

Attention lingering without demanding possession.

Nothing hidden or performed. It was simply there.

Her skin remembers before her mind does.

It has been a long time since Reighn allowed herself to be reckless.

Not that Sloan fails her. Their intimacy is heat without hesitation. Unscripted. Certain. It steadies.

His hands know her without searching.

Her body answers without delay.

There has never been doubt between them — only completion.

Lately something has stirred — a restlessness predictability no longer quiets.

It wasn't desire.

It was the recognition of wanting more than certainty.

"You're thinking too hard," Journey says.

Reighn doesn't deny it.

Journey pours Michter's 20-Year instead of cognac and tells Siri to play Eric Roberson.

Reighn remembers the juke joint. The jock. Journey waving him off like a traffic signal.

"You remember this?" Reighn asks, singing the lyrics.

"Four feet two, even with shoe inserts."

"I still owe you," Reighn says, swaying.

The music slides under her skin, loosening something that has been cinched too tight.

"As long as you owe me," Journey laughs, "I'll never go broke."

Then, softer: "You ever wonder why Sloan doesn't travel with you more?"

"He joins me, sometimes," Reighn says. "But he's got young techs glued to him."

"Riiiiight."

Reighn remembers Sloan by the fire pit. The pipe. The quiet.

The way his mouth lingers when he kisses her goodnight.

The way she has begun to anticipate the end before it arrives.

The way she received him had begun to feel different.

Journey drags a finger along Reighn's arm.

"Where'd you just go — pain or pleasure?"

Reighn doesn't move her arm away.

"Girl, stop being so nosy."

Journey lifts her glass instead of pressing.

"I know what you really need."

"Enlighten me."

"Your ass needs a fuckation."

Reighn snorts. "What the hell is a fuckation?"

"Come with me," Journey says, fanning the invitation. "Unless reckless is just theory."

Reighn drains her glass.

The warmth spreads, but it isn't the bourbon doing it.

Something in her shifts.

Chapter Six

"Inanna has spoken," Journey whispers, scanning the terrace. "A fuckation of grand proportion is exactly what the gods ordered."

She drifts backward before Reighn can respond, already distracted by a broad-shouldered figure cutting through lantern light.

Reighn accepts a flute of champagne and lets her gaze move.

The mansion rises in tiers of glass and carved stone, accordion doors thrown open to a terrace overlooking water she cannot quite see but can feel. Silk brushes skin. Laughter breaks and reforms. Bodies lean into one another without urgency. No one hides. No one performs modesty.

Her obsidian mask rests against her cheekbones as though it belongs there. The asymmetrical lace bodysuit beneath her wrap skirt holds her upright and fluid at once. One arm remains bare. The other veiled. She registers the glances and allows them to dissolve without invitation.

A hand grazes the small of her back as someone passes.

She does not turn.

Music spills through the open doors, bass low enough to settle beneath her ribs. Beyond the outer ring of lantern light, past the easy choreography of guests leaning into one another, she notices a canvas set away from the main terrace near a low stone wall where ivy climbs unchecked.

It is not positioned for viewing.

It is angled slightly inward, as though turned toward itself rather than the party.

She moves toward it.

With each step, the music softens until it feels less like sound and more like vibration. Conversation dissolves into indistinct murmur. Gravel shifts beneath her heels. The air cools, brushed with salt and the faint scent of damp leaves.

By the time she reaches the edge of the garden path, the house feels distant.

The canvas stands several paces beyond the last reach of lantern glow. No spotlight claims it. No crowd surrounds it. It exists without announcement.

Color bends and fractures without spilling. Lines push outward but refuse collapse. Negative space opens at the center, not empty but charged, as though holding breath.

She studies the composition without searching for its maker.

Warmth gathers low in her body and remains there, not urgent, not impatient, simply present.

Only then does she become aware of movement beside the frame.

The artist stands just beyond the edge of shadow, working with deliberate precision. A matte black wrap binds her hair close to her skull. A dark tunic marked with old paint falls straight from shoulder to thigh. Her movements are economical, assured, as though she wastes neither gesture nor thought.

She hums under her breath, something low and unrecognizable.

Reighn steps closer to the canvas.

"What will go there?" she asks, nodding toward the open center.

The woman rinses her brush in a shallow basin, wipes her fingers on linen, and turns slightly.

"I've been waiting."

"For?" Reighn asks.

The woman's mouth curves, not wide.

"For the right interruption."

Reighn lifts her chin, intrigued. "And you think you've found it?"

"Come closer."

Reighn does.

They stand shoulder to shoulder now, close enough that she catches the scent of oil, skin, and something warm that belongs to neither exclusively. Laughter filters faintly from the house. Wind moves along her bare arm.

"You don't fill what doesn't need filling," Reighn says. "That's rare."

"I only complete what asks to be entered."

The air between them tightens, not with urgency, but recognition.

Reighn extends her hand. "I'm—"

"Shhh."

A cool fingertip presses lightly against her lips.

"Rule number three. No names."

The touch lingers just long enough to alter her breathing before retreating.

"First time?" the artist asks.

"Not exactly."

The artist's fingers trace the line of Reighn's collarbone, unhurried, following lace to bare skin. She pauses at the inside of her wrist, pressing gently against the pulse before releasing it, as if confirming something only she can measure.

"Here?" the artist murmurs, fingers grazing the belt at Reighn's waist.

Reighn nods once.

The fabric loosens and slides to the ground.

Cool air meets warm skin.

The artist steps back slightly, studying the angle of shoulder and throat, the line of waist, the way light rests along her hip before traveling downward. Her gaze returns to Reighn's mouth.

"Your form holds light beautifully," she says.

"May I?"

Reighn answers with another nod.

The first stroke lands against her shoulder.

Paint cool against heat.

The brush moves slowly, bristles parting as they glide across skin. The second stroke follows the curve of her collarbone, deliberate and steady. The third dips lower, mapping without claiming.

Reighn feels her breath deepen, not quicken.

The artist steps away and turns to the canvas. One decisive stroke alters the center. The negative space tightens, reshapes, responds.

"You see it," the artist says without turning.

"See what?"

"The part you keep folded."

Reighn's jaw firms slightly.

The brush returns to her skin, this time along the inside of her arm. The artist's free hand steadies at her waist, warm and assured.

"Close your eyes," she says softly.

Reighn does.

She feels the final stroke along her shoulder blade before the brush lifts. Fingers trail once along the curve of her hip, neither hurried nor possessive, and then release her completely.

When Reighn opens her eyes, the canvas is no longer waiting.

The center holds form now, not portrait and not mimicry, but something that feels like entry rather than ornament.

She retrieves her wrap and ties it slowly, aware of the heat that has not dispersed.

"You're not finished," she says.

The artist dips her brush again, gaze steady on the altered composition.

"I am."

Music swells faintly from the house.

Reighn turns toward the terrace, the garden air still cool against her skin.

At the edge of lantern light, she pauses.

The artist has returned to her work, brush moving in measured arcs. As if sensing her there, she glances over her shoulder.

A smile reaches her mouth first.

Two paint-marked fingers lift in acknowledgment.

Reighn does not look away.

Then she steps back into the light.

Chapter Seven

Reighn stands at the kitchen counter, humming under her breath as she stirs honey into tea that has already cooled. Morning light settles against the windowpane. A drop slides onto her index finger and she brings it to her mouth without thinking.

Sweetness lingers.

Her tongue pauses there a moment longer than necessary, and warmth begins to unfurl low and slow, as if something inside her has stretched awake after a long sleep.

She lowers herself onto a stool.

"That must have been some event," Sloan says.

He leans in the doorway, hands tucked into the pockets of his lounge pants, a smile resting easily on his face.

"Good morning," she replies.

He crosses the kitchen, fills the kettle, and measures beans into the grinder. "Coffee?"

She lifts her mug in answer.

He glances at her, then lets his gaze rest a fraction longer than usual, something softer than amusement settling in his expression. "I feel like I should be sending a thank-you card. Maybe flowers.

Last night was different." He stirs cream into his cup. "In all the right ways."

"It was pleasant," she says.

The word feels smaller than the memory.

"Am I the reason for that smile?"

Cool air along her shoulder.

Color drying against skin.

Laughter without explanation.

A mouth that did not hesitate.

Hands that moved without hurry.

"Speaking of late," Sloan says, "shouldn't you be at the studio?"

She checks the time. 07:34.

"Slight adjustment," she replies, already reaching for her bag.

He steps behind her, breath warm against her ear. "Attention to detail matters."

His hand settles at her waist, firm and familiar. He presses his mouth just below her ear, not asking, simply claiming.

A moment later, he pulls back and wipes just beneath her left ear with a napkin before placing it in her palm.

Several colors stain the paper.

Not hers.

"Thank you," she says, brushing a kiss across his cheek. Her mouth lingers there a fraction longer than habit requires.

Her phone rings.

"I'll see you this evening," Sloan calls as he heads upstairs. "Text me when you're done."

"Good morning, Genesis," Reighn answers. "Is everything all right?"

"There's a special delivery. Only you can sign."

"I'm on my way."

In the elevator, she unfolds the napkin and closes her eyes. She lifts it briefly to her nose.

Cedar. Resin. The faintest echo of skin warmed by night air.

***

The studio door is already unlocked.

Two couriers stand with Genesis. Different companies. White gloves. Clipboards.

"This arrived an hour ago," Elberto says. "Instructions were clear. Delivered before nine. Owner must sign in the presence of the courier."

No return address. No sender.

A thirty-by-forty canvas stands upright nearby.

Reighn signs.

"Would you like assistance unwrapping it?" Elberto asks.

"That won't be necessary."

"Come," Genesis says to the couriers. "I'll walk you out."

Their heels fade down the corridor. The door closes.

The room grows still.

Reighn opens the crate.

Glassine.

Charcoal corner guards.

Hand-torn linen tape.

She peels each layer back carefully.

At first there is only atmosphere — warm umbers and breath-thin grays, light shifting through pigment.

Then she sees it.

The tilt of her shoulder in the garden.

Turned. Intentional.

Lace riding high along her hip.

The curve of her waist caught mid-breath.

Where a face might have formed remains untouched.

The body gathers itself without posing.

Her breathing slows.

Of course.

Her fingers rest lightly against the frame, not for balance but to feel it — to confirm that memory has been rendered faithfully.

Something shifts inside her, recognition rather than surprise. The same current that answered when paint first touched her skin.

Her attention drops to the corner.

In the corner, just beyond the sweep of charcoal shadow, something interrupts the surface.

Not a signature.

Not initials.

A single thumbprint pressed into the paint while it was still wet.

It is not centered. Not ornamental. It rests slightly to the side, visible only if one knows to look.

The ridges remain intact.

Deliberate. Unhidden.

She lifts her own hand, turning it slightly, comparing the pad of her thumb to the impression before her.

Recognition lives in the body.

Her fingers hover near the mark, stopping just short of contact.

Footsteps approach.

She does not turn.

Genesis enters first, taking in the canvas with a sharpened gaze. "That's magnificent. Who's the artist?"

Reighn lets her eyes move once more across the line of her own body rendered without apology.

"Oh, shit." Journey stops in the doorway. "That explains everything."

Chapter Eight

The walk from the studio to Bread & Spread is short enough that it never feels like a hike. Only a pause. Just enough time for her body to catch up to what her mind refuses to name.

Her thighs remember before her thoughts do.

Outside Palimpsest, the city keeps its rhythm. Delivery trucks idle with quiet impatience. A cyclist calls out a warning that sounds more courtesy than complaint. Footsteps layer over one another like percussion. Somewhere nearby, a storefront radio leaks old R&B through a cracked door.

The city keeps moving.

Journey suggests food. Genesis agrees immediately, cheeks still flushed, eyes bright with questions she doesn't ask.

"Girl, I did not mean to out your freaky-deak nature to your staff," Journey says as they step onto the sidewalk.

The grin ruins the apology before it lands.

The air smells like warm concrete and coffee grounds rinsed down drains. Sugar lingers—something baked recently, something meant to be shared. Reighn slows without realizing it, adjusting her stride.

The slight pull in her hips makes her more aware of how she is walking.

"There's nothing to apologize for," she says.

Bread & Spread announces itself before the door opens.

Butter and yeast, heat rising behind it.

Inside, warmth holds without crowding. Brick walls softened by steam and years of conversation. Wooden tables scarred just enough to feel earned. Light spills through tall windows, catching flour and dust midair.

"Two," Reighn says to the hostess.

The last open table waits near the back wall.

"My treat," Journey says. "You grab the table. I'll order."

The room hums. Chairs scrape. Ceramic touches saucer. A barista calls out names like she knows the stories attached to them. Ovens exhale.

Fresh bread. Toasted nuts. Dark coffee. Citrus cutting through richness.

Reighn lets it settle.

Her body remains tuned to something else entirely.

Cool air against skin.

Paint drying where fingers had studied her.

The quiet that followed.

The weight of a palm at her waist.

The way her own breath changed without permission.

The gift kept it.

Journey returns with a tray—cast-iron chicken caprese, a Dumbo cheesesteak, shrimp and corn chowder. Reighn splits the sandwiches without discussion, trades halves, shakes pepper into the soup.

"We can share."

Nearby, a couple leans together over one plate. Someone reads with a notebook open beside their mug, pencil resting where it might be lifted at any moment.

The drinks haven't arrived yet.

Journey places the napkins. Straightens the table.

Then she looks at Reighn.

"Before they get here," she says, quieter now, "I need to ask you something."

Reighn stills.

Journey drums her nails on the table.

"Okay, spill it. What really happened in that garden?"

Reighn doesn't look away.

She lets the silence stretch just long enough to enjoy it.

"Grown folk business."

Journey leans back slightly. "Oh, we're playing that card, are we? Well, that's not an answer."

"Actually, it is," Reighn says. "If you must know, Nosy Nancy, it was a very pleasant experience."

Her mouth curves as she says it, remembering exactly how pleasant.

Journey's brows knit; her lip curls. "And?"

Reighn dips bread into the chowder. Takes a few bites.

Chews slowly. Swallows deliberately.

"What happens in the garden stays in the garden."

Journey's eyebrows lift. "Mm-hmm."

"I should be asking you what took place with you," Reighn adds lightly.

Journey adjusts her collar. "It might not have been Vegas, but ya girl did get lucky."

"Ask me no questions," Reighn says, dipping another piece of bread.

"I tell you no lies," they say in unison.

Reighn's smile lingers longer than the joke.

Not secrecy.

Ownership.

Chapter Nine

The room reads like The Row, Lemaire, Jil Sander—quiet luxury worn by people who don't need introductions. That has always been Reighn's intention for *Black Salt*. It was never meant to be spectacle or noise. It was designed for experience.

She doesn't rattle easily.

This morning, she feels it.

Not fear. Not doubt. Something sharper. Anticipation that won't sit still.

Despite breathwork, meditation, tapping—tools she trusts—her nerves refuse to settle. Sloan notices before she says anything. He takes her hands, kisses her palms, and eases her onto the loveseat in her dressing room closet.

"Here," he says gently. "This is a Loewe occasion."

He's right.

The blouse is ivory silk, fluid but substantial, draping cleanly against her frame. The neckline appears severe until movement reveals a quiet asymmetry. Her trousers are deep charcoal wool, high-waisted, precisely tailored. They move when she walks. Nothing clings.

Black Loewe ankle boots. Architectural heel. Matte leather.

A small Puzzle bag in soft tan calfskin. A single gold cuff. Stud earrings she no longer considers.

The mirror agrees.

She looks composed. She does not feel contained.

"Let me take that," Genesis says, reaching for her bag. "Now go. Mingle. Drink. Relax."

Genesis hugs her once, quick and sincere, then disappears into the office.

The room hums with its own authority—curators, collectors, musicians, actors who move through museums the way others move through clubs. Reighn spots Thelma Golden beside Robert Glasper, their heads inclined toward a Julie Mehretu that vibrates with motion. Across the room, Sloan laughs at something Erykah Badu says. Reighn lifts her glass to him. He grins back.

Even as a child, she never imagined this.

Artists. Admirers. Patrons.

One room.

She reaches for another flute — and stops.

The noise carries on.

Her focus doesn't.

The woman stands before El Anatsui's piece without drifting.

The leather A-line dress fits close through the shoulders and torso, widening at the skirt. Matte. Structured. It absorbs light instead of reflecting it.

Her expression as she studies *Tethered Currents* is the same one Reighn wore the first time she saw it.

They stand beside one another, allowing the sculpture to hold the space.

"Don't you love how he reclaims material?" the woman says, eyes still on the piece. "It never feels nostalgic. Just honest."

"Tethered Currents," Reighn replies.

The woman smiles. "Exactly."

Reighn turns toward her.

Smooth skin, bronzed by unhurried sun. Eyes suspended somewhere between jade and amber. Locs gathered into a loose bun that suggests intention without fuss. The leather A-line dress fits close through the shoulders and torso before widening cleanly at the skirt. Matte. Structured. It absorbs light instead of reflecting it.

There is something measured about her stillness. Not stiffness. Not reserve. Presence.

Reighn searches her memory the way she searches a catalog, not for a face but for placement. Openings blur together over the years. Studio visits. Private previews. Artist dinners in cities that begin to resemble one another when viewed from hotel windows.

Nothing settles.

"My friends call me Misha," the woman says, turning fully now.

They shake hands.

Her grip is steady and warm. She does not hurry the release. A faint press of her thumb at the inside of Reighn's wrist before their hands part, subtle enough that it might have been accidental.

Reighn lowers her hand slowly, aware of the place without looking at it.

Genesis appears at her side.

"My apologies for interrupting," she says, resting a light hand on Reighn's arm. "There's a situation that needs your attention."

Reighn nods. "Excuse me."

They move through the room. Hans Ulrich Obrist. Terrace Martin. Jeffrey Wright. Genesis slows once. Reighn gives a small shake of her head.

Inside the adjacent display room, the sound softens.

"The Akunyili Crosby is still in bonded storage in Newark," Genesis says. "It cleared London on schedule. Customs hasn't released final clearance."

Reighn glances at the crowd through the open door. Sloan lifts his chin in her direction. She nods, then smiles. He returns his attention to Thelma, who lowers her voice to a whisper, then snaps it bright again, drawing out each word until laughter breaks loose around her. "Change of plans," Reighn says.

Genesis scrolls, recalculating.

"Bring Calder forward," Reighn says, turning toward the door.

Genesis' finger hovers above the tablet. "The Calder statue?"

"Yes."

Genesis sets the tablet down—lighting cues shift, handlers move, a quiet recalibration.

"Handled," she says.

Reighn nods once and steps toward the doorway.

Journey barrels toward her, heels striking hard, eyes wide.

"There you are! Girl, you gotta see what's going on."

She grabs Reighn by the wrist and pulls.

Reighn steadies herself, half a protest forming—

The painting stands near Sloan.

Unassuming in placement.

Commanding in presence.

Her breath catches — once.

Heat flashes up her spine before she can mask it.

That wasn't for sale.

A swell moves through the room — not for the painting, but for the sculpture now lit at center stage.

Bronze catches light.

A murmur rises.

"Will the artist be joining us?" Hans Ulrich Obrist asks, angling his head toward the sculpture.

Reighn blinks. "I'm sorry?"

"You were just speaking with her," he says. "Artemisia Calder."

The name lands intact.

Reighn turns.

The space where Misha stood is empty.

The room hums on.

At center stage, the Calder sculpture catches its light. Bronze deepens under the wash, shadows carving muscle and motion from stillness. A murmur moves outward, low and appreciative — the kind reserved for work that doesn't ask permission.

Genesis appears beside the platform, already holding a microphone.

"Before we continue," she says, her voice carrying easily across the room, "I'd like to take a moment."

Conversations taper. Glasses lower. The lights remain warm but focused.

"*Black Salt* has always been about experience over spectacle," Genesis continues. "About choosing work that speaks for itself. Tonight is the result of that vision."

She turns toward Reighn.

"Please join me in honoring the founder of *Black Salt.*"

Genesis lifts her flute.

The room follows.

Glass catches light.

Applause rolls through the space.

Reighn presses her hand to her collarbone and smiles.

Sloan meets her with a bouquet — dozens of white peonies bound in simple cream ribbon.

He presses them into her hands. "You did that," he says quietly.

His fingers graze the inside of her wrist — the same place Misha touched.

She leans into his embrace, then steps toward the microphone.

"Thank you," she says. "Thank you for trusting the work."

She lifts her glass.

"This is *Black Salt.*"

The room rises with her.

And she stands in it.

Chapter Ten

"Gurl, when I say you did the damn thing—you did it."

Journey's voice bursts through the phone. Even without speaker, a couple passing by glance over as she laughs.

Reighn keeps walking.

Black Salt had surpassed even what she'd budgeted for. Each click of her heels lands clean against the pavement.

Her body feels newly calibrated, as if something inside her has shifted its center of gravity.

"I mean it," Journey continues. "First Inanna. That alone would've made my year. But then add me chopping it up with Robert Glasper and my girl, Tina—"

An ambulance cuts down the street, siren splitting the moment. Reighn lifts a hand to her ear until it fades.

"Oh, so now you're on a first-name basis with Beyoncé's mama?" she says.

Journey laughs. "Don't hate the player. Only thing missing was Mickalene Thomas."

Reighn slows.

Mickalene Thomas doesn't just enter rooms.

She alters them.

"That's a good idea," Reighn says. "I'll make a note."

"Now where are we celebrating?" Journey presses. "Champagne brunch. My treat."

Reighn reaches the studio door—and stops.

Door's ajar.

No text message from Genesis. No missed call. Besides, she'd given her the morning off.

"Hey," she says quietly. "I'm at the studio. Door's unlocked. I'll call you back."

A van idles at the curb.

George's Express — Fine Art.

Elberto sits behind the wheel. He lifts a hand. She returns it.

"I'll call you back," she repeats, and ends the call.

Inside, nag champa, vanilla, and nutmeg hang in the air.

Underneath it, something warmer. Familiar.

Voices echo.

"Genesis?" she calls.

"Back here."

The lighting is dimmer than usual. Reighn flips the switch.

"And that's the last signature," Genesis says, handing back a stylus. "Thank you for coming on short notice."

Reighn steps further inside.

On the sofa sits the woman from the night before.

She looks comfortable. Waiting.

Reighn searches for the name.

Artemisia. As in Gentileschi.

"Artemisia," Reighn says.

Misha rises, then steps closer.

"S'il te plaît," she says lightly. "Call me Misha."

Please. Call me Misha.

Reighn takes her hand. The contact is steady.

Warmer than it should be.

"Reighn," she replies. "You may call me Reighn."

Misha repeats it. The name rests easily between them.

Her accent curves around it, softening the edges.

Reighn's gaze moves across the room.

Everything looks in place. Her walls.

The work.

Then—

The easel.

Empty.

"The painting," Reighn says. "Where is it?"

Genesis hesitates. "Ms. Badu requested it. She felt it belonged beside the sculpture."

Silence.

"It's… where?" Reighn asks.

"Already in transit."

The feeling settles low in her body.

Not anger. Possession.

That piece hadn't been listed. It hadn't been offered.

It had been sent to her.

Misha lifts her bag. "I can step out."

"No," Genesis says, the word landing before she can soften it. "Please stay."

Genesis rubs her thumb along the edge of the stylus. "I understood it as an extension of the installation."

"It was," Reighn says, her voice low. "We'll address it later."

Genesis nods once, then turns to Misha. "It was very nice to meet you. And thank you again for coming in on such short notice."

Once Genesis shuts the door, the studio quiets.

Misha steps beside Reighn. They face the empty easel.

"That painting," Misha says, "was extraordinary. Whoever created it understands intimacy without spectacle."

The clock ticks.

Reighn turns slightly toward her.

Misha steps closer.

Close enough that the air between them changes.

"Je peux te montrer un endroit…" she says softly.

I can show you a place…

She doesn't look away.

"Où ces couleurs respirent."

Where these colors breathe.

Reighn's pulse shifts.

"Il n'y a aucune obligation," Misha adds evenly. "Prends ton temps."

There is no obligation. Take your time.

She slips a card onto the table.

"Mon numéro est là."

My number is there.

A pause.

"À toi de voir."

It's up to you.

Reighn says nothing.

Her silence is not uncertainty. It is consideration.

Misha studies her for a moment longer.

“Je serai en ville jusqu’à jeudi.”

I’ll be in the city until Thursday.

She turns toward the door.

At the threshold, she pauses just long enough to call down the hall, “Genesis—thank you again.”

The door closes behind her.

The studio quiets.

Reighn walks to the window.

Below, Misha steps onto the sidewalk.

She does not rush.

A plane cuts across the afternoon sky.

Reighn watches until it disappears beyond the skyline.

Heat settles again, patient and deliberate.

Chapter Eleven

"I guess if someone was going to receive a painting of your naked body, it should be Ms. Low Down Loretta Brown herself."

Journey hasn't stopped laughing.

"I've got an old Polaroid she can have for free."

She fluffs the pillow behind her back and tucks her legs beneath her. "I hope you went easy on Genesis. You know she's softer than she lets on."

Reighn opens the fridge and begins assembling a charcuterie board—goat cheese, aged cheddar, olives slick with oil, thin folds of cured meat.

Her movements are unhurried. Deliberate.

"Genesis meant no harm," Journey says. "Who could blame her? The painting was extraordinary. Anyone would have wanted it."

"I'm glad you're entertained," Reighn says. "Now grab a bottle from the wine fridge."

Journey selects a Provence rosé and uncorks it.

"Perfect," she says, setting out two glasses.

They step onto the balcony—Journey with the wine and glasses, Reighn with the board. The afternoon stretches wide. Sunlight across water. Birds circling. A saxophone rising from somewhere below.

"So," Journey says, tone shifting, "tell me about this Senegal situation. And this mystery artist."

"I don't know very much," Reighn says, refilling her drink.

And yet she feels as if she knows exactly enough.

"Me either, other than she's named after two legends and creates fantastic sculptures."

Reighn sips. "Someone has been Googling."

Journey waves off the comment.

"Not any two artists, either. Two powerhouses," Reighn says, placing a piece of cheese onto a cracker. "Artemisia Gentileschi and Alexander Calder."

A flock of geese fly overhead.

"So, it's her actual name?" Journey asks. "And not a fancy pen name?"

Reighn nods as she refills their glasses.

"And Sloan?" Journey asks.

"He'll be out of the country."

"Colombia again?"

Reighn returns to the kitchen to refresh the platter.

"That's his third trip this year," Journey says, watching her. "You're not curious?"

"Not in the least," Reighn says, placing the tray back on the table.

Her tone holds. Steady.

Journey studies her a beat, then smiles.

"I would've gone with you," she says, emphasizing the word I. "But Thiago has claimed my calendar."

Reighn laughs. "Who should be interrogating whom?"

Journey leans closer. "When I say that man handles his business…"

"Girl," Reighn says, tilting her head.

"Girl," Journey says, scooting towards the edge of her seat, elbows resting on her knees.

Her grin turns wicked.

"Girl." Reighn's expression widens.

They dissolve into laughter.

The breeze shifts.

"I know you don't need permission," Journey says, quieter now. "But you deserve something that fills you too."

Reighn meets her eyes.

The word fills lands somewhere deeper than it should.

"I don't need permission," she says.

Journey grins. "I know."

She presses a kiss on Reighn's cheek.

"You're painting again. And Senegal might stretch you in ways this place can't."

Reighn looks out over the water.

She imagines heat that doesn't cool when the night ends.

After a moment, she nods.

"Too bad you can't take Garden Girl with you," Journey says lightly. "You might come back glowing."

Reighn's mouth curves.

She already feels altered.

"Help me with these dishes," Reighn replies. "Before you say something you can't unsay."

Chapter Twelve

"Bienvenue au Sénégal, ma chère."
Welcome to Senegal, my dear.

Misha greets Reighn with a light kiss on both cheeks, smiling as they lift her luggage into the trunk.

Her lips linger a fraction longer on the second kiss.

"How was the flight?" Misha asks once they're buckled in. "Are you hungry?"

The eight-hour journey has left Reighn loosened more than tired.

Her body feels unguarded in a way it hasn't in years.

"Not yet," she says. "But soon."

The road unfurls from Blaise Diagne International Airport, wide and sun-washed. The Atlantic rides the wind. The sky hangs pale and high. Bougainvillea flashes pink against low buildings. The radio hums with mbalax, its rhythm settling into the roll of the tires.

Color moves without apology.

Women in wax-print dresses walk along the roadside with baskets balanced on their heads. Vendors lift trays of oranges and peanuts when traffic slows. Motorbikes slip between lanes. Goats wander without urgency.

"You weren't exaggerating," Reighn says. "The colors breathe here."

As they enter Dakar, the air thickens—charcoal smoke, grilled fish, salt. Buildings draw closer. The sea flashes steel-blue between palms and concrete.

"Dakar is living art," Misha says.

Reighn watches, saying nothing.

The city presses against her senses without asking for permission.

"I hope you love seafood," Misha adds. "Every meal will include fish."

"That sounds perfect."

She thinks of thiéboudienne—spiced fish and rice stained red with tomato. Street stalls. Linen-draped tables open to salt air. Oil, heat, citrus.

"I want to go to Gorée," Reighn says after a moment. "If it's half as powerful as it looks…"

Misha's expression shifts.

"Prépare-toi."

Prepare yourself.

"I plan to."

Misha's hand finds hers briefly.

Her thumb presses once against the inside of Reighn's palm before releasing.

"I know you love Brooklyn," Misha says. "But here, art isn't separate."

She gestures toward the street.

"Issa Samb turned life into performance. Alioune Diagne paints our memory. Kalidou Kassé. Fatou Kiné Diakhaté. We carry them."

The names settle between them.

Reighn watches a woman pass in a dress the color of marigolds, the fabric lifting in the wind while a boy runs behind her, laughing. Fishermen pull their nets from the water with practiced hands, the rhythm steady and unhurried.

Her ribs expand—not from calm, but from something opening.

She looks out at the horizon, then back at the city rising behind her.

Misha's gaze lingers along her profile. She doesn't reach for her phone. She doesn't reach for anything at all.

Chapter Thirteen

Reighn meets her gaze in the mirror.

She wears a sleeveless linen midi dress in muted clay-rose—the color of earth after rain. The fabric shifts when she moves, skimming her hips before settling again. A shallow V frames her collarbone. The skirt brushes her calves when she turns.

Flat leather sandals ground her—thin straps, no heel, built for walking.

Her hair is loose. Soft against her shoulders.

Music plays low from her phone on the dresser. Something warm and percussive. A steady rhythm that settles into her hips without asking permission.

A knock at the door.

Misha stands there when she opens it, smiling.

"No first night in Dakar would be complete without an LBD—little black dress—moment," she says, though she's wearing indigo and brass instead.

When they checked in, Misha had mentioned she'd taken the room next door.

"Tour guide and bodyguard," she'd said.

Reighn hadn't pressed.

Now Misha looks composed and certain in a way that suggests she understands exactly how the evening might unfold.

Her two-piece is hand-dyed ankara and indigo batik—wax print layered with intention. One shoulder bare. The other draped. High-waisted trousers move easily when she steps inside. Brass cuffs catch the light. Cowrie-shaped earrings shift as she tilts her head.

The music continues to hum.

"You started without me?" Misha asks lightly.

Reighn shrugs. "I don't like silence when I'm getting ready."

Misha steps fully into the room and closes the door behind her. The latch clicks softly.

"I bought the fabric in Plateau," she says, turning slightly so the indigo catches the light. "It was plain cotton once."

Even her sandals are handmade. Built for streets. Built for moving.

"And I have something for you."

She pulls a small indigo pouch from her bag, tied with gold cord. Inside are sculptural brass ear cuffs, curved to follow the natural line of the ear. No two exactly alike.

Misha steps close enough that Reighn can feel her warmth before her hands rise.

She fits the first cuff carefully, her fingers steady against Reighn's skin. Then the second. Reighn watches in the mirror as metal warms along the curve of her ear.

Misha's fingertips linger, brushing the shell of her ear, sliding down the line of her jaw before easing away.

"I bought them in Medina," she says quietly. "A young metalsmith. Recycled brass. Lost-wax casting. She works by feel."

Her fingertips skim the side of Reighn's neck when she tucks a curl behind her ear. "No two are the same."

Reighn tilts her head slightly. Light traces the new lines of metal against her skin.

"You can't order them," Misha adds. "You have to come here."

"They're beautiful," Reighn says.

"They're meant to be worn," Misha replies, her gaze lowering briefly to Reighn's collarbone before lifting again.

The music shifts to something slower.

Misha glances toward the phone, then back at Reighn.

"Do you dance before you go out," she asks, "or only after?"

Reighn smiles faintly. "Depends on who I'm with."

Misha steps closer.

"Show me."

She reaches for Reighn's hand and draws her gently away from the mirror, toward the open space near the window. The curtains lift slightly with the night air.

Their fingers interlock.

The rhythm is slow enough that they don't need to think about it. Reighn's free hand settles at Misha's shoulder. Misha's palm rests at Reighn's waist, the contact firm and deliberate.

They begin to move.

Not performance.

Not rehearsal.

Just a slow shifting of weight from foot to foot.

Misha draws her closer until their hips align. Reighn feels the heat of her through linen and indigo. The space between them narrows without urgency.

Misha's thumb traces a small, absent circle at the curve of Reighn's waist.

"You came for the country only?" she asks softly.

"Only?" Reighn repeats.

Misha's mouth hovers near her ear. "And for me."

The words brush her skin.

Reighn turns her head slightly. Their faces are inches apart now.

"I came for both," she says.

Misha's hand slides slowly down Reighn's arm, fingers tracing the length to her wrist before weaving back into her hand. She lifts it and presses her lips to the inside of Reighn's palm.

Not rushed.

Not playful.

Intentional.

Reighn's breath shifts.

Misha draws her in again, her mouth brushing the curve beneath Reighn's ear, lips grazing skin in a slow line toward her neck. Her hand tightens slightly at Reighn's waist as if to steady them both.

Reighn's fingers slide into the back of Misha's hair, holding her there for a moment longer than necessary.

The music continues.

Outside, the city hums.

Inside, their bodies move in a slow rhythm that has nothing to do with the speaker.

When they separate, the air feels altered.

Misha studies her face.

"We should go," she says, though neither of them steps away immediately.

"Yes," Reighn answers.

They release hands only long enough to open the door.

The night greets them warm and watchful.

As they walk toward the elevator, their fingers brush again.

This time, neither pretends it was accidental.

Reighn doesn't feel dressed.

She feels awake.

Chapter Fourteen

The night air hangs warm against the terrace, wind moving through the open atrium and lifting the edge of indigo silk at Misha's hip. Music drifts from somewhere beyond the wall, low drums threading into the quiet of the courtyard.

Reighn adjusts the strap at her shoulder and smooths the linen at her waist. The city hums faintly beyond the gate.

"You're ready?" Misha asks.

Reighn turns toward her and pauses long enough to take her in. The fabric wraps her hips, one shoulder bare, brass catching the low light. The scent she wears—cedar and something brighter beneath it—settles between them.

"Yes," Reighn answers.

They walk toward the gate together. Just before Misha reaches for the latch, she stops and takes Reighn's wrist, guiding her gently to the side where the stone wall shields them from the street.

"Once we leave this building," Misha says quietly, her hand sliding from wrist to waist, "we dance."

Reighn studies her face. "And when we return?"

Misha steps closer until fabric brushes fabric and warmth replaces air between them. "When we return," she says, her thumb tracing the curve beneath linen, "we don't."

The kiss begins slowly, a measured brush of lips that feels deliberate rather than stolen. Reighn's breath catches before she steadies it. Misha deepens the kiss without hurry, pressing closer, her hand tightening just enough at Reighn's waist to anchor her there. Reighn's fingers slide into Misha's hair and hold her in place for a beat longer than necessary.

When they separate, neither moves away immediately. Misha rests her forehead against Reighn's and lets her thumb drift once along her jaw.

"This will last," she murmurs, her mouth still close enough that the words graze skin. "Until we come back."

Reighn swallows, eyes steady. "I'll hold you to that."

Misha smiles and opens the gate.

***

Nioko Klub pulses before they step inside. The bass moves through Reighn's ribs and settles into her hips as light shifts across skin and fabric. Bodies fill the room, moving in rhythm without spectacle. No one performs. No one hunts for attention. The energy belongs to whoever claims it.

Misha keeps her hand at the small of Reighn's back as they move through the crowd. The touch reads as dance, but the pressure of her palm says otherwise. Reighn lets her own hand travel up the length of Misha's arm, fingers sliding deliberately from wrist to shoulder before easing away.

They dance close, hips aligning, shoulders brushing, breath warming skin whenever they lean in to speak. Misha's mouth hovers near Reighn's ear.

"You feel it?" she asks.

"Yes."

Their fingers interlock briefly when the rhythm shifts, separating only when someone turns between them. Misha's thumb presses lightly into Reighn's waist, and Reighn responds by drawing her hand slowly along the slope of Misha's back, mapping her through fabric without breaking the boundary they agreed to.

The tension isn't loud. It's contained.

When the music swells, Misha leans close enough that her lips nearly touch Reighn's cheek. "Later," she says softly.

Reighn meets her gaze. "Yes."

They dance until sweat gathers at their collarbones, and the rhythm settles into muscle memory.

When they step back onto the street, the night presses close, humid and electric. A taxi idles near the curb, windows down, music humming softly from its speakers.

Misha lifts her hand and the driver pulls forward immediately.

They slide into the backseat, knees brushing. The door shuts with a hollow thud and the car eases into motion.

The driver glances at them through the rearview mirror, one eyebrow lifting slightly at the way they're both still flushed.

"Nioko treated you well?" he asks in French-accented English.

Misha laughs first. "It tried."

The driver grins. "It always tries."

Reighn leans back, still warm from dancing. "The drums tonight felt different."

"Friday," the driver replies. "The good percussionists come out on Fridays. They show off."

"They did," Reighn says.

Misha turns toward her, smile widening. "You were the one showing off."

"I was responding."

"To me?"

"To the music."

The driver chuckles softly, shaking his head. "Music and women," he says. "Always the same answer."

Reighn laughs, low and unguarded, surprising even herself.

The city moves past in streaks of amber and shadow, vendor stalls resting dark behind their shutters as motorbikes weave between lanes. Somewhere along the coastal stretch, salt air slips in through the open windows.

Misha's hand rests on Reighn's thigh, casual enough to pass for balance as the taxi rounds a corner.

"You disappeared for a minute," Misha says quietly. "When that song shifted."

Reighn turns her head slightly. "I didn't disappear."

"You left your body."

Reighn smiles faintly. "I found it."

The driver hums along to his radio, unbothered.

When they reach the gate, Misha leans forward to pay before Reighn can reach for her bag.

"Come back tomorrow," the driver says. "Same rhythm."

Misha smiles. "We might."

The door opens. Warm air rushes in.

The glass doors slide shut behind them.

The lobby hums softly with late-night arrivals and muted television light behind the reception desk. Marble floors hold the echo of their steps as they move toward the elevators.

Inside the mirrored car, no one else joins them.

This time, Misha does not wait.

Her hand returns to Reighn's waist, guiding her gently against the brushed steel wall as the elevator begins its slow ascent. Her mouth finds Reighn's again, deeper now, slower, the kiss no longer shaped by an audience. Reighn exhales against her lips as Misha's fingers slide along the curve of her hip.

"You made me wait," Misha murmurs.

"You said it would last," Reighn replies.

The elevator hums steadily upward.

The glass doors slide shut behind them.

The lobby hums softly as they cross toward the elevators. Inside the mirrored car, no one joins them.

The doors close.

This time, Misha does not wait.

Her hand settles at Reighn's waist, turning her gently toward the wall as the elevator begins its slow ascent. Her mouth finds Reighn's again, deeper now, slower, the kiss no longer shaped by an audience. Reighn exhales against her lips as Misha's fingers slide along the curve of her hip.

"You made me wait," Misha murmurs.

"You said it would last," Reighn replies.

The elevator hums steadily upward.

When the doors open onto their floor, they separate just enough to move down the hallway without spectacle.

Outside Reighn's door, Misha reaches for her again, not hurried, not asking. Her hand traces once along Reighn's jaw before she leans in for a final kiss, softer this time but no less deliberate.

"And tomorrow," Misha says quietly, "you come to me."

"Tomorrow," Reighn answers.

Misha steps back and disappears into the suite next door.

Chapter Fifteen

Morning comes in through open shutters and the steady breath of the Atlantic.

Reighn wakes first.

Light spills across the linen sheets in wide bands, warming the curve of Misha's shoulder where the blanket has slipped. One arm stretches above her head, fingers relaxed, mouth softened by sleep. Her breathing moves deep and even.

Reighn traces the line of Misha's collarbone with her eyes, the small scar near her rib, the steady rise and fall of her chest. She leans down and presses her mouth to the inside of Misha's wrist.

Soft.

Not enough to wake her.

Then she slips from the bed.

Later, when she steps onto the terrace, the garden waits below—wind bending low grasses, dark stone paths cutting through open air, sculptures rising in quiet authority against the sea.

Salt gathers on her lips.

She tastes it.

"I didn't hear you leave the bed."

Misha's voice carries from behind her.

Reighn turns.

Misha stands barefoot in the doorway, fabric loose against her hips, hair unbound.

"You looked so peaceful," Reighn says. "I didn't want to wake you."

Misha holds her gaze, then crosses the terrace.

Her hands settle at Reighn's waist, thumbs pressing into the curve just above her hips. She leans in slowly, her mouth finding the place where shoulder becomes neck.

Reighn's breath deepens.

Reighn turns in her arms without breaking contact, her hands sliding up Misha's ribs, thumbs brushing the underside of her breasts before settling at her back. She pulls her closer, closing the last inch of space between them.

Misha lets her breath linger there, close enough to blur the space between them.

Their lips meet.

Not searching.

Landing.

Misha's fingers thread into Reighn's hair as Reighn's hand slides down to the back of her thigh, lifting her slightly so their hips align.

Salt. Skin. Morning air.

They part only when breath demands it.

Misha rests her forehead against Reighn's.

"Come," she says quietly.

Inside, the villa holds light differently than Brooklyn. Air moves freely. Concrete floors cool beneath their feet. The studio door opens and the temperature shifts—cooler, denser with pigment and turpentine softened by oil.

An easel waits in the center of the room.

A stone palette flecked with dried color. Jars of brushes clouded with old pigment. Tubes folded from use.

Misha walks to the windows and pushes them wider. Music drifts in from somewhere beyond the walls—low percussion, patient and steady.

She turns back to Reighn.

"Les sculptures sont pour le monde," she says, touching the edge of a chisel resting on a shelf. "Mais la peinture…" Her eyes remain steady. "C'est intime."

Reighn steps forward.

Misha picks up a brush, dips it into ultramarine, draws a single wavering line across the blank canvas, then places the brush in Reighn's hand.

Their fingers remain intertwined around it for a breath longer than necessary.

Reighn lifts the brush and makes her own mark—firmer. Ochre crosses blue. The color deepens where it meets resistance.

Misha reaches past her for sienna.

Their shoulders brush.

Neither moves away.

Misha's hip settles briefly against hers before shifting, but Reighn turns into it this time, pressing back deliberately.

A streak of paint lands across Reighn's forearm.

Misha laughs.

Reighn answers by dragging her paint-slicked thumb across Misha's collarbone, leaving a bold swipe of gold against dark skin.

Misha inhales.

The laughter fades.

The space narrows.

Paint gathers on wrists, along jawlines, beneath fingernails.

Color builds on canvas in broad, instinctive strokes. Lines resist symmetry. Space opens where it needs to.

Reighn steps back, measuring the balance between tension and release.

Then she sets the brush down.

Misha watches.

"Peins-moi," she says.

Paint me.

Misha reclines on the chaise near the window. She removes her dress slowly, not performing, simply freeing skin from fabric. One arm tucks behind her head. The other rests along her thigh, palm open.

Light travels along her body in long bands.

Reighn does not reach for the brush.

She steps forward instead. Her hand finds Misha's ankle and slides upward along the length of her calf, over the back of her knee, up the inside of her thigh until her palm settles at her hip.

Misha's fingers flex at her side.

Reighn bends and presses her mouth to the hollow beneath Misha's ear. Not tentative. Not asking. Her lips linger there before traveling down the curve of her neck.

Misha's fingers close in her hair.

At the same time, Misha draws her closer, their hips meeting fully, paint transferring from one body to the other.

Reighn's thumb presses into the soft space at Misha's waist.

Their mouths meet again.

Slower.

Deeper.

When they part, it is not from reluctance.

Reighn reaches for a clean brush.

Now she paints.

She traces shadow first—where collarbone dips, where rib meets breath. She deepens the hollow of the throat. Warms the curve of hip with sienna and gold.

Misha does not pose.

She remains open, present, breathing through each pass of bristle and skin.

"Comme tu me vois," she murmurs.

As you see me.

Reighn moves between canvas and body, mapping light, committing curve to pigment, letting instinct guide her hand.

Her knuckles brush Misha's stomach as she leans in.

Misha arches into the touch.

The Atlantic strikes stone below.

Inside, paint moves in slow, deliberate strokes.

Time loosens.

Color builds until the canvas holds both body and breath.

When Reighn steps back, the room feels altered.

Misha rises and crosses to her.

She lets the painting settle in her eyes before turning to Reighn.

Painted fingers trace the curve of Reighn's jaw, then down to her collarbone, following the path her mouth traveled earlier.

"Merci," she says softly.

Reighn reaches up and cups the back of her neck.

This time, when their lips meet, there is no hesitation.

Outside, the garden bends toward the sea.

Inside, something long folded has opened fully and does not close again.

Chapter Sixteen

The gallery smells faintly of fresh paint and cut wood. Shipping crates line one wall, names stenciled beneath layers of tape. Assistants move with quiet focus, lifting, measuring, adjusting without waiting to be told. Outside, trucks idle along the curb. DUMBO hums. The Manhattan Bridge rises through the glass like steel drawn across sky.

In three days, the doors will open.

Journey paces the length of the room in heeled boots that have no business on raw wood floors.

"I still can't believe you were in Senegal for fourteen days and didn't call me once," she says, not for the first time. "I would've FaceTimed you from the damn tarmac."

Genesis catches Reighn's eye over a clipboard, one brow lifted.

Reighn only says, "Help me move that easel. I want the Mickalene to anchor this wall."

Even wrapped, rhinestones glint through protective paper. When the covering falls away, the portrait ignites—legs open, chin lifted, gaze steady and unconcerned with approval.

"Is that a—"

"Tschabalala," Reighn answers as another piece is revealed beside it. Fabric collides with paint, hips cut wide, limbs reassembled without apology.

Journey stops in front of a Toyin Ojih Odutola portrait and folds her arms.

"These women look like they know something," she says. "Like they're not explaining themselves to anybody."

"They aren't," Genesis replies.

Reighn steps closer to adjust the track lighting. As she reaches up, brass flashes against her skin. The sculptural cuffs at her ears catch and hold the gallery light for a beat before warming back into shadow.

Journey notices. Says nothing.

Genesis notices. Says nothing.

Sloan, entering with a crate balanced against his hip, notices and looks longer.

"Did someone leave a package here?" he asks.

The crate is larger than the others. No return address. French printed clean across the label.

Reighn feels it before she speaks.

Genesis scrolls through her tablet. "We're not expecting Simphiwe until next week."

"It looks important," Sloan says, setting it down carefully.

Reighn nods once.

The crowbar slides beneath the lid. Wood splinters. Nails release.

Inside: two canvases.

Numbered.

"Start with one," Sloan says.

Glassine peels back.

Journey inhales sharply. "Shit just got real."

The Garden.

Reighn stands barefoot in gold light, paint streaked across her hands, wind lifting her hair as if it knows her name.

"There's writing on the back," Sloan says, turning it slightly. "Celui-ci remplace celui qui a trouvé preneur."

Genesis leans in. "This replaces the one that found a buyer."

Reighn does not answer.

"Open the other," Journey says, voice lower now.

The second canvas emerges.

Misha reclined in the grass. Nude. Unarmored. Watching.

Reighn seated before her, brush steady, body unhurried. The Atlantic rising behind them in deep cobalt and burnished gold.

Across the front, near the lower corner, just above the thumbprint pressed into the paint, hand-lettered in deliberate script:

The Taste of Her

Journey freezes.

The brass at Reighn's ear glints again.

Journey steps closer, eyes darting between the thumbprint and the painting.

"Oh, Sookie, Sookie, now," she breathes.

Genesis studies the lower corner, then looks at Reighn.

"It was her," she says quietly. "All along."

No one rushes to fill the silence.

"Translate the rest," Journey says.

Reighn turns the canvas just enough to read the inscription on the back. Her finger traces the ink as she speaks.

"The woman I saw in the garden was the woman you have always known yourself to be. This canvas is only proof. She has always been there. In you. With you. It was never just the art, my love. It was you."

The words settle into the room without resistance.

Sloan steps behind her, his hands settling lightly at her shoulders, thumbs brushing the fabric at her collarbone. He stays.

"You're hanging them," he says.

"Yes."

"Together?"

"Yes."

He nods once. His fingers skim upward briefly, grazing the brass at her ear before falling away.

An assistant approaches. "Where would you like your pieces placed?"

Reighn turns.

"My pieces?"

The assistant gestures toward the opposite wall.

Her work waits there.

Large-scale canvases layered in indigo and rust. Salt pressed into pigment. Sand embedded in oil. Shoulders squared. Spines unbent. Mouths closed—not silenced, simply uninterested in permission.

Genesis steps back as Journey goes quiet, and Sloan moves with her.

Reighn crosses the room and lifts the first canvas onto the center hook. She adjusts the corner by a fraction, steps back, then forward again, ensuring the line of sight holds.

The woman in the painting meets the empty gallery head-on.

No plea in her mouth.

No apology in her stance.

Journey exhales. "The collectors are going to lose their damn minds."

Genesis smiles. "About time."

Assistants resume moving. Tape tears. Ladders shift. Instructions fly. Outside, Brooklyn pulses.

Reighn stands at the center.

Mickalene blazing on one wall.

Tschabalala wide and unapologetic beside her.

Toyin layered in graphite shadow.

Misha's *Garden* burning gold beneath its title.

The thumbprint pressed into gold.

Her own women anchored in salt, skin, and refusal.

She lifts her hand once, adjusting the brass at her ear. The metal warms beneath her fingers.

Assistants move around her. Tape tears. Ladders shift. Brooklyn hums beyond the glass. The room no longer feels borrowed.

When she was small, she had said it with a certainty that unsettled the room — that one day they would be paying for it. The adults had smiled. Some had laughed. Mimi had not.

Mimi had only taken her face in both hands and told her not to let anyone name her small. Not to let anyone soften her edges to make themselves comfortable. Not to confuse love with limitation.

Reighn had listened.

She chose her work the way some people choose safety—deliberately and without apology. She chose the hunger that kept her awake at night, the walls she would someday stand inside, the life that would expand instead of narrow. She chose the man who stands behind her without trying to rename her, and she chose the taste that now carries her name because she built it there.

In three days, the doors will open and the room will fill, not with noise but with recognition. Collectors will drift closer than they intended to. Critics will study longer than they planned. Conversations will soften at the edges as the work begins to speak for itself. Checks will be written not out of curiosity or spectacle, but because what stands on these walls refuses to be dismissed.

No one handed her this room. No one rescued her into it. Every inch of it exists because she decided, years ago, that what lived inside her would not be made smaller for anyone's comfort.

Reighn does not step aside.

She stands in the space she made, and it fits her the way it always promised it would.

Epilogue

Journey presses her forehead to the taxi window like she's eight years old and somebody just handed her a passport.

"I swear," she says, squinting, "if one more goat walks past like he pays rent, I'm negotiating with somebody's grandmother."

Reighn laughs.

Dakar moves outside the glass in color and rhythm. Dust rises in soft spirals. Music carries from somewhere unseen. A woman passes with mangoes stacked high on her head as if she were born with a crown. A boy runs barefoot behind a rolling tire, hollering at nothing and everything at once.

Journey exhales slowly.

"Okay. Now this? This is different."

"You said that in Brooklyn," Reighn replies.

Journey turns her head. "No. I said your bare walls were about to make you act brand new. Do not remix my quotes."

They step out near the sculpture garden along the Corniche.

There is no signage, no spotlight, no velvet rope.

Only wind.

Salt thick in the air. The Atlantic breathing like it has never once concerned itself with anyone's deadlines.

Journey stops walking.

The bending figure catches her first — the woman arched toward the sea.

"Oh."

Reighn doesn't interrupt.

Journey steps closer, studying the bronze curve.

"She's not falling," she says after a moment. "She's—"

She tilts her head.

"She's offering."

Wind lifts the edges of their dresses. Hair brushes against cheeks. Somewhere behind them someone laughs in Wolof, the sound bright and passing.

They move slowly past fractured columns and bodies caught mid-gesture, metal shaped into motion that never quite finishes.

"You know what's wild?" Journey says. "Back home, if you stand still too long somebody thinks you're depressed."

"And here?" Reighn asks.

"Here it feels like you might finally hear yourself."

They sit on the low wall overlooking the water.

The waves do not perform. They arrive, meet stone, and withdraw, steady in a rhythm older than anything built along the shore.

Journey leans back on her palms.

"Okay," she says softly. "This… I understand."

Reighn looks down at her left hand.

A faint line marks where something used to rest. The skin has adjusted, but it remembers.

The wind moves through her hair, and she lifts her face toward the horizon.

The smile that settles there is not practiced or presented. It rests easily, like it belongs.

The sun lowers, turning the Atlantic molten.

Goats wander past as if the road answers to them.

Music rises somewhere behind them, folding into wind and salt.

The breeze shifts, carrying cedar first, then something brighter, warmth beneath it — familiar enough to register without demanding to be named.

Reighn keeps her eyes on the line where the water meets the sky.

She does not turn.

Journey bumps her shoulder lightly. "You good?"

Reighn exhales, the sound quiet and certain.

"I am."

And she means it.

ABOUT THE AUTHOR

Aiken Ponder writes character-driven fiction rooted in psychological depth and restrained heat. Her stories explore identity, autonomy, and the charged moments when control loosens and recognition takes its place. Neither traditional romance nor thriller, her work lives in the tension between discipline and desire. She writes to explore the quiet moments that change everything.

ALSO BY AIKEN PONDER

80 Days of Pleasure (Days of Pleasure Series Book 8)

It Lied Between Us

The Day She Stopped Participating

The Safe Place Was a Lie

Queen of Belize (Queen of the Castle Book 4)

NEXT BOOK PREV

Coming Soon from Aiken Ponder

The Safe Place Was a Lie

There are rules for surviving.

Breathe slow.

Observe everything.

Never assume safety.

Solace thought she understood danger. She knew how to read rooms, measure silence, track the shift in a voice before it hardened. She knew how to endure.

What she didn't know was that the most dangerous spaces don't announce themselves.

They welcome you.

When Solace is taken to a private residential facility designed for "restoration," she's told it's temporary. Therapeutic. Necessary. The language is gentle. The doors are not.

Inside, the air hums with compliance. Schedules replace choice. Conversations are monitored. Smiles linger a second too long. The staff call it care.

But Solace notices the gaps.

Missing records.

Changed stories.

Patients who disappear without explanation.

A twin who feels almost right — but not entirely.

The rules shift.

Trust no comfort.

Question every kindness.

Survive long enough to understand the pattern.

As systems tighten and loyalties fracture, Solace realizes the truth isn't hidden in what she sees — but in what's absent. And once she recognizes it, there's no returning to who she was before.

Because the most terrifying realization isn't that you're trapped.

It's that the place built to protect you was never safe at all.

A psychological thriller about control, misdirection, and engineered inevitability.

Facebook: https://www.facebook.com/AuthorAikenPonder/

Instagram: https://www.instagram.com/aiken_ponder/

https://wordstoponderpublishing.com/aiken-ponder

www.ingramcontent.com/pod-product-compliance
Lightning Source LLC
Chambersburg PA
CBHW010020260726
48782CB00033B/535

* 9 7 9 8 8 9 6 6 4 0 1 8 9 *